DISNEY'S
THE
LION KING

Illustrated by the Disney Storybook Artists
Adapted by Kate Hannigan

Visit our Web site at www.disneybooks.com
Disney Enterprises, Inc.

Published by
Louis Weber, C.E.O.
Publications International, Ltd.
7373 North Cicero Avenue
Lincolnwood, Illinois 60712

www.pilbooks.com

Manufactured in China.

8 7 6 5 4 3 2 1

ISBN: 0-7853-9546-6

All the animals of the Pride Lands gathered on the plains to welcome the Lion King's cub into the world. The cub's name was Simba. Rafiki, the wise baboon, carried Simba to the top of Pride Rock and held him high for all to see. The animals cheered. They knew that Mufasa and Sarabi's cub would one day be king.

Only one lion refused to celebrate Simba's presentation. It was Mufasa's brother, Scar, who was angry that he would never rule. Mufasa climbed to the cave where Scar sat alone. He reminded his brother that Simba wasn't just Mufasa's son, he was Scar's future king!

Mufasa loved Simba, and they shared many adventures. On a special morning, they watched the sun rise over the African plains.

"One day, Simba, the sun will set on my time here and will rise with you as the new king," Mufasa said as they looked out at the fields of gold. Everything the light touched would be Simba's to rule. Everything, that is, except the shadowy place.

The Lion King warned Simba about the shadowy place. He told him that he must never go there.

Mufasa tried to teach his cub many things. He wanted Simba to understand the difference between right and wrong, and to respect every creature in the kingdom. "We are all connected in the great circle of life," Mufasa said.

One afternoon Simba saw his uncle and told him he was going to be a great king when he grew up. Simba boasted that he was going to rule the whole kingdom. "Everything except that shadowy place," he said, remembering what his father taught him. Simba told Scar he was not allowed to go there.

Scar was always up to no good, and he saw an opportunity to make trouble. So he told Simba lies about the shadowy place. Scar told Simba about the elephant graveyard there. He told him that only the bravest lions went to the elephant graveyard.

Simba wanted to be brave, just like his father. Simba ran off to tell his friend Nala what Scar had said. He wanted to go to the shadowy place right away to prove how brave he was.

Simba found his friend Nala playing near their mothers. He whispered to Nala so their mothers wouldn't overhear. Simba knew his mother would be very angry if she heard that he wanted to go to the shadowy place.

Simba and Nala tried to sneak away, but it was clear they were up to something. Their mothers told Zazu, the Lion King's feathered adviser, to watch over the young cubs. As Simba and Nala ran off toward the forbidden land, they tried their best to lose Zazu.

Simba and Nala jumped and played along the trail. They tumbled down a hillside and landed smack in the shadowy place. It was the elephant graveyard!

"It's really creepy!" Nala said.

"It sure is," Simba said. "Come on, let's check it out!"

Zazu caught up with the cubs and warned them it was dangerous. But it was too late! Three sinister hyenas crept out of the shadows. The cubs took off running, but the hyenas chased them. Simba and Nala were cornered!

At the last moment, there was a mighty roar. It was Mufasa! He chased the hyenas away and saved the two young lion cubs.

Mufasa was angry with his young cub. He told Zazu to take Nala home—he was going to teach Simba a lesson. Simba felt terrible. He was sorry he disobeyed his father. Simba told him he just wanted to be brave, the way Mufasa was.

Mufasa said he was only brave when he had to be. "I was scared today when I thought I might have lost you," he told Simba. They hugged, and Mufasa's anger finally left him. Simba was proud of his father for scaring away the hyenas, and he felt better now.

Simba climbed upon Mufasa's strong back. He felt safe and happy. They would always be together, Simba thought to himself.

Mufasa looked up at the beautiful night sky filled with bright stars. He told Simba that the stars were the great kings of the past looking down on them. "Just remember," Mufasa said, "those kings will always be there to guide you. So will I."

Scar was angry at the hyenas after they ran from Mufasa. They had let Simba and Nala escape! So Scar devised another plan, and this one was even more terrible than the first. Scar wanted nothing more than to make himself the Lion King!

Scar lured Simba to the center of a deep gorge and told him to wait for a special surprise. Simba loved surprises. The young cub paced excitedly.

Then Simba heard a low rumble, and felt the ground begin to shake. It was a herd of raging wildebeests! The hyenas had caused a stampede!

    Simba jumped onto a tree branch, but he was losing his grip. Suddenly, Mufasa appeared and rescued Simba. Mufasa carried his cub and set him safely on a high rock.

    But Mufasa slipped on the jagged rocks and hurt himself. As he tried to climb to safety, he called to Scar to help him. But Scar refused to help his brother.

    Mufasa slipped back down the rock. He was gone.

    The wicked Scar wanted to be king so badly. Now, the one thing in his way was Simba. He had to get rid of him too.

Scar blamed his nephew for hurting Mufasa. Simba said it was all an accident. Scar knew it wasn't Simba's fault, but he was deceitful.

"Run away, Simba, and never come back!" said Scar.

Simba was afraid and sad. He didn't know what to do, so he ran and ran. He didn't stop until he was deep in the desert. He was tired and thirsty. Two friendly animals—a meerkat named Timon and a warthog named Pumbaa—found him and gave him water.

They asked Simba what was wrong, but Simba wouldn't tell them. They tried to cheer up the miserable lion cub by teaching him hakuna matata—"no worries." Timon and Pumbaa said he should put the past behind him. Simba tried to do just that. And after a little while, it actually helped.

The lion cub felt happy with his new friends. They spent their days splashing in the water, relaxing in the grass, and gazing up at the stars.

The days went on and Simba grew and grew. He looked more and more like his father every day.

One afternoon, Timon and Pumbaa were searching for food when another lion appeared. She was hungry and hunting for her lunch. It was Nala! Simba recognized her right away. He was so happy to see her.

Nala was surprised to see her friend. She said that since Simba was alive, he was the Lion King. Simba wanted to keep the past behind him. He said he wasn't the king.

Nala told Simba how terrible things had become under Scar's rule. She said Simba was the only hope the animals had to save the Pride Lands. Simba was confused. He needed a sign, something to show him what he should do. That's when Rafiki, the wise old baboon, appeared.

Rafiki, the
baboon, led Simba
on a chase through
the jungle. The old
baboon was up to
something. Finally,
they reached a pond of
still, clear water.

Simba gazed down into the water. He saw his reflection and the twinkling of stars. Hearing his father's voice, Simba looked up into the night sky. There amid the bright stars, he saw Mufasa's face!

Mufasa told Simba to look inside himself. It was the sign Simba was looking for. "You are the one true king," his father told him. "Remember who you are. Remember."

Simba knew he would have to face his past. He was ready. Simba raced through the jungle, running on and on until he reached the Pride Lands. He found that the trees had turned brown and dry, and the grasses were no longer green and lush. Things were very bad. He would make them better, he thought to himself.

Nala caught up with him, and Timon and Pumbaa, too. They vowed to fight together.

Simba searched the rocks for his uncle. Scar was shocked by the sight of his nephew, who was no longer a helpless little cub. Scar thought the powerful lion before him was Mufasa back to haunt him.

Simba challenged Scar, saying the wicked ruler could either step down as Lion King or fight. Scar loved power and wanted to rule the land, so he ordered his hyenas to attack. As the hyenas jumped toward Simba, the other lions protected him and chased the hyenas away.

Scar would have to fight Simba himself. The two lions battled fiercely. They pounced up and down the rocks, wrestling and growling. After a long fight, Simba pinned Scar down and forced him to admit to all the lions what he had done so many years ago. Scar finally told the lions that it was his fault, not Simba's, that Mufasa was gone.

"Run away, Scar! Run away and never come back!" called Simba, finally ridding the kingdom of the wicked Scar.

The lions cheered Simba's return to the Pride Lands.
Finally Simba was able to take his rightful place as the
Lion King.

As Simba climbed to the top of Pride Rock, he
remembered all that his father had taught him. He let out
a mighty roar, and the lions answered. Nala stood beside
Simba as his queen. And just as he did so many years ago,
Rafiki held up the Lion King's cub for all to see.

A new circle of life was begun.